# What I Think
# You Need To Know....
# And Why You Should Care

Nicole Cherie Higgins

# DEDICATION

This Book is dedicated to anyone and everyone who has a sense of humor , or does not. It doesn't Fu*king matter.

# CONTENTS

## Chapters

26 ...

27 ......

28 .......

29 ....

30 .....

31 .......

32 .....

33 ......

34 ......

35 ......

36 .....

37 .....

38 ........

39 ...

40 .......

41 .....

42 .......

43 ......

44 ....

45 .....

46 .........

47 ......

48 ...

49 .....

50 ......

51 .....

52 .....

53 .....

54 .....

55 …..

56 ………

57 …….

58 …..

59 ……

60 …….

61 …..

62 …..

63 …….

64 ……

65 …..

66 ……..

67 …….

68 …….

69 ………

70 …..

71 ……

72 …..

73 ……

74 ………

75 …….

76 …..

77 ……

78 …..

79 …….

80 ……..

81 …….

82 …….

83 ……..

84      ……..

85      ………..

86      …..

87      ……

88      ………

89      ……..

90      ……..

91      ……..

92      ……….

93      …………………………

# CHAPTER 1
# WHAT YOU NEED TO KNOW

What you need to know is this;

THE WORLD IS CRAZY.

# CHAPTER 2

# CHAPTER 3

# CHAPTER 4

# CHAPTER 5

# CHAPTER 6

# CHAPTER 7

# CHAPTER 8

# CHAPTER 9

# CHAPTER 10

# CHAPTER 11

# CHAPTER 12

# CHAPTER 13

# CHAPTER 14

# CHAPTER 15

# CHAPTER 16

# CHAPTER 17

# CHAPTER 18

# CHAPTER 19

# CHAPTER 20

# CHAPTER 21

# CHAPTER 22

# CHAPTER 23

# CHAPTER 24

# CHAPTER 25

# CHAPTER 26

# CHAPTER 27

# CHAPTER 28

# CHAPTER 29

# CHAPTER 30

# CHAPTER 31

# CHAPTER 32

# CHAPTER 33

# CHAPTER 34

# CHAPTER 35

# CHAPTER 36

# CHAPTER 37

# Chapter 38

# Chapter 39

# Chapter 40

# Chapter 41

# Chapter 42

# Chapter 43

# Chapter 44

# Chapter 45

# Chapter 46

# Chapter 47

# Chapter 48

# Chapter 49

# Chapter 50

# Chapter 51

# Chapter 52

# Chapter 53

# Chapter 54

# Chapter 55

# Chapter 56

# Chapter 57

# Chapter 58

# Chapter 59

# Chapter 60

# Chapter 61

# Chapter 62

# Chapter 63

# Chapter 64

# Chapter 65

# Chapter 66

# Chapter 67

# Chapter 68

# Chapter 69

# Chapter 70

# Chapter 71

# Chapter 72

# Chapter 73

# Chapter 74

# Chapter 75

# Chapter 76

# Chapter 77

# Chapter 78

# Chapter 79

# Chapter 80

# Chapter 81

# Chapter 82

# Chapter 83

# Chapter 84

# Chapter 85

# Chapter 86

# Chapter 87

# Chapter 88

# Chapter 89

# Chapter 90

# Chapter 91

# Chapter 92

# Chapter 93

# ABOUT THE AUTHOR

This book has been brought to by Nicole Cherie Higgins. You may remember her from such epic novels as, the one I never wrote part 1, the one I never wrote part 2, and the finale the one I never wrote….part 3. You probably never read them, because I probably didn't write them…yet, but that's no excuse to not have read them.

Nicole Cherie Higgins is a person that lights up any room, you know like the Illuminati. I'm not saying that I am the illuminati but, I never said I wasn't either. Are you scared right now? Don't be because unlike that blood thirsty fellowship, I am an artist who does art. Like paintings and stuff. Like an artist. And I sell stuff on Amazon cuz I'm a seller as well. I'm motivated. I hustle. Why don't you? You should. Speaking of selling stuff, you should check out my store in Amazon. N.A.B.S. For real you should check it out. I got good stuff. Check it out.

I'm also a Life Coach. I have like 17 certifications. CLC certified. I also am permanent makeup artist. For reals. I'm like certified. I'm not gonna list them all out because that's too many to list because you'd be reading about my certifications all day because I have mastered everything beauty. Because I hustle. Again. Why don't you?

You might be asking yourself how did we come up with this book. Well, I will tell you right now in all seriousness.

Me and my esteemed co-author Brian went on a  Little trip to the desert.  While there he brought up a conversation he had with someone important who was in desperate need of his guidance. He proceeded to tell me the story and his conversation went like this, "The world is crazy." I sat there waiting for the next part of the story. There was none. That was it.

Though  it might be such a simplistic, small, short saying and it certainly does not sound like it's the ending of a conversation, really, it sums up just about everything possible in life. No matter what situation or what event or what crazy, weird, funny, sad, mad, happy, etc etc etc , " things" happen to us, it all boils down to just knowing one simple thing. The world is crazy. And this might just be a crazy idea for a book but I felt like it fit right in with the worlds crazy. Thank you for having a sense of humor and reading this book. I hope the reading wasn't too long. Be on the look out for the second book coming out very soon!